The Wind in the Willows

The Wind in the Willows

KENNETH GRAHAME

Condensed and adapted by
Clay Stafford

Illustrated by
Nick Price

Cover illustrated by
Laura Fernandez
Rick Jacobson
sharpshootersinc.com

Dalmatian Press

The Dalmatian Press Great Classics for Children
have been adapted and illustrated with care and thought,
to introduce you to a world of famous authors, characters, ideas,
and stories that have been loved for generations.

Editor — Kathryn Knight
Creative Director — Gina Rhodes
And the entire classics project team of Dalmatian Press

THE WIND IN THE WILLOWS
Copyright © 2004 Dalmatian Press, LLC

The DALMATIAN PRESS name and logo are trademarks
of Dalmatian Press, LLC, Franklin, Tennessee 37067
No part of this book may be reproduced or copied in any form
without the written permission of Dalmatian Press.

ISBN: 1-40371-011-2 (M) 1-40371-386-3 (X) 1-40371-867-9 (M2)
13563

06 07 08 09 LBM 15 14 13 12 11 10 9 8 7 6

A note to the reader—

A classic story rests in your hands. The characters are famous. The tale is timeless.

This Great Classic for Children by Dalmatian Press has been carefully condensed and adapted from the original version (which you really *must* read when you're ready for every detail). We kept the well-known phrases for you. We kept the author's style. And we kept the important imagery and heart of the tale.

Literature is terrific fun! It encourages you to think. It helps you dream. It is full of heroes and villains, suspense and humor, adventure and wonder, and new ideas. It introduces you to writers who reach out across time to say: "Do you want to hear a story I wrote?"

Curl up and enjoy.

DALMATIAN PRESS
GREAT CLASSICS FOR CHILDREN

ALICE'S ADVENTURES IN WONDERLAND

ANNE OF GREEN GABLES

BLACK BEAUTY

THE CALL OF THE WILD

THE STORY OF
DOCTOR DOLITTLE

HEIDI

THE ADVENTURES OF
HUCKLEBERRY FINN

A LITTLE PRINCESS

LITTLE WOMEN

MOBY DICK

OLIVER TWIST

PETER PAN

POLLYANNA

REBECCA OF SUNNYBROOK FARM

THE SECRET GARDEN

THE TIME MACHINE

THE ADVENTURES OF
TOM SAWYER

TREASURE ISLAND

THE WIND IN THE WILLOWS

THE WONDERFUL WIZARD OF OZ

CONTENTS

1. The River Bank.. 1

2. The Open Road... 15

3. The Wild Wood 29

4. Badger's Home 41

5. Home Sweet Home.. 55

6. Mr. Toad... 69

7. The Protector of Small Creatures 85

8. Toad's Adventures... 95

9. Wanderers All... 109

10. The Further Adventures of Toad 125

11. The Fall of Toad Hall...................................... 143

12. The Return of Toad 159

About the Author.. 181

CHARACTERS

MOLE — (Moly) a rather shy fellow who leaves his underground home to stay with Ratty on the River Bank

WATER RAT — (Ratty) a friendly River Banker who enjoys boating, good company, and picnic lunches

TOAD — a rich, jolly fellow who tends to brag and go "overboard" when it comes to boats, gypsy wagons, and fast motorcars

BADGER — a wise, quiet fellow in the Wild Wood who prefers to stay away from Society, but always takes care of his friends

OTTER — another friend from River Bank

PORTLY — Otter's young son who wanders off

THE HEDGEHOGS — two agreeable young lads who stop in at Badger's house

CHARACTERS

THE TOOT-TOOT — the motorcar that fascinates Toad and fills him with glee

JAILER'S DAUGHTER — the young lady who has a soft spot for Toad and helps him escape from jail

WASHERWOMAN — the stout woman who switches clothes with Toad, so he can be disguised as the washerwoman

ENGINE DRIVER — the train engineer who helps Toad escape the law

BARGE WOMAN — the barge driver who recognizes Toad for the fool he is

GYPSY — a traveling man who agrees to sell a horse to Toad

WEASELS, STOATS, AND FERRETS — wily, thieving fellows from the Wild Wood who take over Toad Hall

CHAPTER ONE

The River Bank

The Mole had been working very hard all morning spring-cleaning his little home. First with brooms, then with rags, then with a brush and a pail of whitewash. Spring was moving in the air above, filtering down even to his dark little house beneath the soil. It was no wonder, then, that he suddenly flung down his brush and said, "Hang spring cleaning!" Something in the air up above was calling to him.

He hurried out of the house, through a steep little tunnel, muttering "Up we go!" till at last, pop! his snout came out into the sunlight and he found himself rolling in the warm meadow.

"This is fine!" he said to himself. "Better than whitewashing!" He scampered across the sunny meadow till he reached the hedge on the far side.

It all seemed too good to be true. Hither and thither through the meadows he rambled busily, finding birds building, flowers budding, leaves thrusting. And instead of feeling badly for not doing his work, he somehow felt jolly. After all, the best part of a day off is not so much resting yourself, but to see everyone else busy working.

He thought his happiness was complete, when suddenly he stood by the edge of a flowing, sparkling river. He'd never seen a river before. He sat down, enchanted.

A dark hole in the opposite bank just above the water's edge caught his eye. Something bright twinkled down in the heart of it. Then, as he looked, it winked at him, and so declared itself to be an eye. A small face appeared. A brown face, with whiskers. A round face with a twinkle in its eye. With small neat ears and thick silky hair.

It was the Water Rat!

The two animals stood and eyed each other.

"Hullo, Mole!" said the Water Rat.

"Hullo, Rat!" said the Mole.

"Would you like to come over?" asked the Rat.

"Oh, it's all very well to *talk*," said the Mole, from across the flowing river.

The Rat said nothing, but untied a rope and pulled on it—and then lightly stepped into a little blue boat. It was just the size for two animals.

The Rat rowed rapidly across, tied up the boat, and held out a paw to Mole. Soon the Mole found himself actually seated in the back of a real boat.

"This has been a wonderful day!" said Mole. "Do you know, I've never been in a boat before."

"What?" cried the Rat, openmouthed. "It's the *only* thing. Believe me, my young friend, there is nothing—absolutely nothing—like simply messing about in boats. Simply messing," he went on dreamily. "Messing—about—in—boats—"

"Look ahead, Rat!" cried the Mole suddenly.

It was too late. The boat struck the opposite bank full force. The Rat landed on his back at the bottom of the boat, his heels in the air. He picked himself up with a pleasant laugh.

"Ah, yes, there's nothing like a day in a boat. Look here! If you've got no other plans this morning, supposing we drop down the river together, and have a long day of it?"

The Mole wiggled his toes and leaned back on the cushions. "*What* a day I'm having!" he said. "Let us start at once!"

"Hold on a minute." The Rat slipped into the hole in the bank and returned with a lunch basket.

"What's inside?" asked the Mole.

"A picnic. There's cold chicken," replied the Rat. "Coldhampicklesrollslemonadegingerale—"

"Oh, stop," cried the Mole. "This is too much! You must think me very rude, but all this is so new to me. So—this—is—a—River!"

"*The* River," corrected the Rat, as he rowed. "It's my world, and I don't want any other."

"But isn't it a bit *dull* at times?" the Mole asked, dragging a paw in the water. "Just you and the river, and no one else to pass a word with?"

"Dull?" asked the Rat patiently. "Never. The bank is so crowded nowadays that many people are moving away altogether. All day long there's always someone wanting you to *do* something!"

"What lies over *there*?" asked the Mole, waving a paw toward a woodland that darkly framed the water meadows on one side of the river.

"Oh, that's just the Wild Wood," said the Rat. "We River Bankers don't go there."

"Aren't they—aren't they very *nice* people in there?" asked the Mole a bit nervously.

"W-e-ll," replied the Rat, "let me see. The squirrels are all right. *And* the rabbits—some of 'em. And then there's Badger. Dear old Badger! Of course—there—are—others. Weasels—and stoats—and foxes. They're all right, in their way, but you can't really trust them, and that's the fact."

"And beyond the Wild Wood?" asked the Mole.

"Beyond the Wild Wood comes the Wide World," said the Rat. "I've never been there, and I'm never going. Neither will you, if you've got any sense. Now then! Let's have lunch."

The Rat brought the boat alongside the bank, tied the boat, and helped Mole safely ashore.

Mole excitedly shook out the tablecloth and arranged the lunch, saying, "Oh, my! Oh, my!"

After they had eaten a little, Rat asked the Mole, "What are you looking at?"

"I am looking," said the Mole, "at a streak of bubbles traveling along the surface of the water."

A broad glistening nose showed itself above the bank, and the Otter hauled himself out.

"Greedy beggars!" he said. "Why didn't you invite me, Ratty?"

"This was an unplanned event," explained the Rat. "By the way—my friend Mr. Mole."

"Pleased to meet you, I'm sure," said the Otter.

There was a rustle behind them, coming from a hedge, and a stripy head with high shoulders behind it peered out at them.

"Come on, old Badger!" shouted the Rat.

The Badger turned his back and disappeared.

"That's *just* the sort of fellow he is!" said the Rat, disappointed. "Stays to himself. Well, tell us, Otter, who *is* out on the river?"

"Toad's out, for one," replied the Otter. "In his new wager boat. New outfit, new everything."

The two looked at each other and laughed.

"First he took to sailing," said the Rat, "then it was flat-bottomed boats. Last year it was house-boating. Now a wager boat. He gets tired of one thing and starts something new."

"No stability," remarked the Otter wisely.

Just then a wager boat flashed into view. The rower—a short, stout fellow—splashed badly and rocked a good deal. The Rat stood up and called to him, but Toad—for it was he—shook his head.

"He'll be out of the boat in a minute," said Rat.

The Otter chuckled—and then slipped away.

"I suppose *we* ought to be moving on," said the Rat. "I wonder which of us had better pack the lunch basket?"

"Oh, please let me," said the Mole, which he did.

The afternoon sun was getting low as the Rat rowed gently homeward, murmuring poetry-things over to himself. The Mole shouted with delight, "Ratty! Please, *I* want to row!"

"Wait till you've had a few lessons."

The Mole, without comment, jumped up and grabbed the oars. The Rat was taken by surprise and fell backward off his seat with his legs in the air for the second time.

"Stop it, you *silly* fruitcake!" cried the Rat. "You'll have us over!"

The Mole flung the oars back—and missed the water altogether. His legs flew up and he found himself lying on the top of the upended Rat. Then over went the boat!

Oh my, how cold the water was to Mole! Oh, how *very* wet it felt! It sang in his ears as he went down, down. Then a firm paw gripped him by the back of his neck. The Rat pulled the helpless animal to shore, hauled him out, and set him down on the bank, a squashy, pulpy lump of misery.

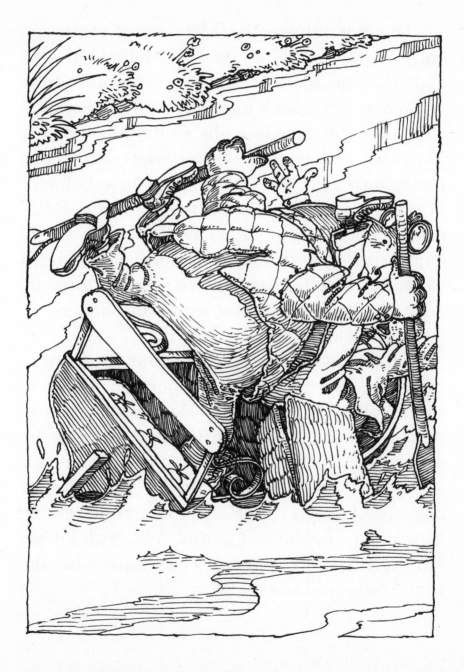

The Rat rubbed the Mole down a bit, and laughed, saying, "Now, then, old fellow! Trot up and down the bank as hard as you can till you're warm and dry again while I dive for the basket."

When Rat had brought everything up, the Mole took his seat in the back of the boat. "Ratty, I'm so sorry. Will you let things go on as before?"

"What's a little wet to a Water Rat?" responded the Rat. "I really think you would enjoy visiting with me for a time. My home is plain, but I could teach you to row and to swim. Soon you'll be as handy as we River Bankers."

The Mole humbly accepted.

When they got to the Rat's home, the Rat told the Mole river stories till suppertime. But very shortly afterward, a terribly sleepy Mole had to be led upstairs to the guest bedroom where he soon fell fast asleep.

This day was only the first of many similar ones for Mole. As spring and summer moved on, he learned to swim and to row. And, with his ear to the river reeds, he often could hear what the wind whispered among them.

CHAPTER TWO

The Open Road

"Ratty," said the Mole suddenly one bright summer morning, "I want to ask a favor."

The Rat was sitting on the River Bank singing a little song. He had just written it, so he was quite delighted with it. Since early morning he had been swimming in the river with his friends the ducks. And when the ducks stood on their heads, suddenly, as ducks will, he would dive down and tickle their necks—just under where their chins would be if ducks had chins. The ducks would come to the surface, spluttering, shaking their feathers at him. So now the Rat sat on the River Bank in the sun, singing his song which he called:

DUCKS' DITTY

All along the backwater,
Through the rushes tall,
Ducks are a-dabbling,
Up tails all!

Ducks' tails, drakes' tails,
Yellow feet a-quiver,
Yellow bills all out of sight
Busy in the river!

Slushy green undergrowth
Where the fish swim—
Here we keep our pantry,
Cool and full and dim.

Everyone for what he likes!
We like to be
Heads down, tails up,
Dabbling free!

High in the blue above
Hawks sail and call—
We are down a-dabbling,
Up tails all!

"I don't know that I think so *very* much of that little song," said the Mole slowly. "But what I wanted to ask you was, won't you take me to call on Mr. Toad?"

"But of course! Let's get the boat out!"

And they were off, with Mole rowing and Rat settled at the back. Rounding a bend in the river, they came in sight of a handsome old house of ancient red brick with well-kept lawns.

"There's Toad Hall," said the Rat. "Toad is rather rich, you know, but very friendly. Not too clever. And he does tend to boast. But he's a fine fellow. Since he has given up boating, I can't wait to learn his new fad!"

"Hooray!" Toad cried, jumping up from his chair on seeing them. "This is splendid!" He shook their paws warmly, and danced about them, without waiting to be introduced to the Mole.

"Delightful residence," remarked the Mole.

"Finest house on the river," boasted Toad.

The Rat nudged the Mole. Toad saw him do it and turned very red. There was silence. Then Toad burst out laughing. "All right, Ratty! That's just my way. But now, you've got to help me!"

"With your rowing, I suppose," said the Rat.

"Oh, pooh! Boating!" said Toad in great disgust. "Sheer waste of time, that's what *that* is. No, I've found the real thing to do with my life. Come see!"

He led the way to the stable yard. There sat a shiny new gypsy wagon brightly painted yellow.

"There's real life for you," cried the Toad. "Life on the open road! Through wilderness and towns! The whole world before you! The finest camper ever built. Planned it all myself, I did—with fold-up beds, a table, and food. We'll have everything we need when we make our start this afternoon."

"I beg your pardon," said the Rat slowly.

"Now, dear good old Ratty," said Toad, "don't be sniffy. You know you've *got* to come!"

"I'm not coming, and that's flat," said the Rat. "I'll stick to my river. And Mole's going to stick with me and do as I do, aren't you, Mole?"

"Of course I am," said the loyal Mole. "All the same, it sounds as if it might have been—well—"

The Rat saw what was passing in the Mole's mind. Toad watched both of them closely.

"Come along and have some lunch," Toad said, "and we'll talk it over. Of course, *I* don't really care. I only want to give pleasure to you fellows. 'Live for others!' That's my motto."

During lunch, Toad was his jolly self, talking of the joys of life on the road. And *somehow* the gypsy wagon adventure became a settled thing.

The happy Toad let his friends round up the old gray horse while he loaded hay in the wagon. Then they set off, all talking at once. It was a golden afternoon. Birds whistled. Travelers called out, "Good day!" Waving rabbits said, "Oh, my! Oh, my!"

Late that night, miles from home, Toad climbed into bed and said, "This is the *real* life for a gentleman! You talk about your old river!"

"I *don't* talk about my river," replied the Rat. "But I *think* about it," he said sadly, "all the time."

The Mole whispered, "I'll do whatever you like, Ratty. Shall we run off in the morning and go back to our dear old hole on the river?"

"No, no," whispered the Rat. "I should stick by Toad. It wouldn't be safe for him alone. This trip won't last long. His fads never do. Good night!"

And indeed the trip did not last long.

The Toad slept soundly—well into the next morning. The Rat fed the horse, lit a fire, cleaned the dishes, and got things ready for breakfast. The Mole hiked off to the nearest village for milk and eggs that Toad had forgotten to pack. By the time Toad awoke to eat the breakfast, the hard work had all been done. He stretched and groaned, "This *is* the gentleman's life!"

They had a pleasant ramble that day, over hills and along country lanes. That afternoon they came out on the highroad, and there disaster struck. They were strolling down the road, when from far behind them they heard a faint hum like the buzz of a bee. A small cloud of dust was approaching—quickly! From out of the dust a "Toot-toot!" sound called out. In an instant, a blast of wind and a whirl of sound made them jump! A magnificent motorcar, with a driver hugging the wheel, flung a blinding cloud of dust—then disappeared, a far-off bee once more.

The horse reared in fright. The gypsy wagon teetered—and then that yellow wagon, their pride and joy, collapsed into the ditch—wrecked!

The Rat danced in the road, shaking his fists. "You villains! I'll report you—you road hogs!"

But Toad just sat down on the dusty road, stared blankly, and murmured, "Toot-toot!"

The Mole managed to quiet the horse, which took some time. But the wrecked wagon was indeed a sorry sight—panels and windows smashed, axles hopelessly bent, one wheel off. The Rat hurried to help the Mole up-end the wagon. "Hey! Toad!" they cried. "Come help us!"

Toad never answered. He sat in a trance with a happy smile on his face. His eyes were still fixed on the dusty spot ahead.

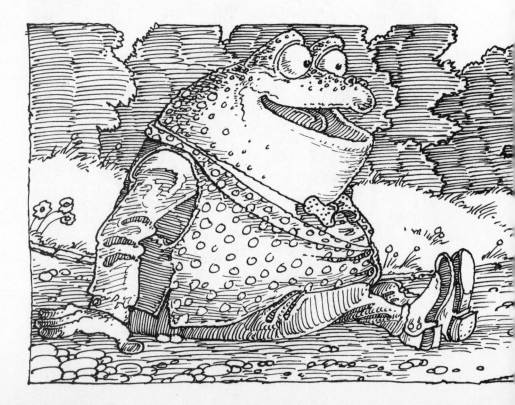

"Are you coming to help us, Toad?" the Rat demanded sternly.

"Glorious sight!" murmured Toad. "The *real* way to travel. The *only* way. O toot-toot!"

"Oh, *stop* being a fool, Toad!" cried the Mole.

"To think I never *knew*!" Toad exclaimed.

"What are we to do with him?" asked the Mole.

"Nothing at all," replied the Rat firmly. "He's got a new craze. He'll continue like this for days now, in a happy dream—quite useless for anything. Come on! The wagon can't be fixed. We'll walk to town."

"What about Toad? We can't leave him!"

"Oh, *bother* Toad," said the Rat.

They had not walked far, however, before Toad caught up with them.

"Now, look here, Toad!" said the Rat. "You'll have to go to the police station—to complain."

"Police station!" sighed the dreamy-eyed Toad. "Me *complain* of that beautiful car? Oh, Ratty!"

"I give up," the Rat said to the Mole. "When we get to town we'll go straight to the railway station. With any luck we'll join a train that'll get us back to the River Bank by tonight."

Upon reaching the town, they left the horse at a stable and hired a man to recover the wrecked wagon. Eventually, a slow train landed them at a station not far from Toad Hall. Rat and Mole led a spellbound Toad to his home. Then they got into their boat and rowed down the river.

That night, the Rat and the Mole dined within their own cozy riverside parlor.

The following evening the Mole was sitting on the bank fishing when the Rat came strolling along to find him.

"Heard the news?" the Rat asked. "Toad went up to town by an early train this morning. He's ordered a large and expensive motorcar."

CHAPTER THREE

The Wild Wood

The Mole had long wanted to meet the Badger face-to-face, but whenever he mentioned his wish to the Water Rat, the Rat would say, "Badger'll turn up someday."

"Couldn't you invite him here?" asked the Mole.

"He wouldn't come," replied the Rat simply.

"Well, then, supposing we visit *him*?"

"He wouldn't like that at *all*," said the Rat. "Besides, he lives in the middle of the Wild Wood."

"You told me the Wild Wood was all right."

"But we won't go there today," replied the Rat. "It's a long way and Badger wouldn't be home. It's summertime. He'll be coming along."

The Mole had to settle for this, but the Badger never came along. During the summer, the Mole found other things to keep him entertained. But when fall came, and then winter, and cold and frost and soggy mud kept them much indoors, the Mole found himself thinking again of the mystery of the solitary gray Badger.

In the wintertime the Rat slept a great deal. During his short day he sometimes scribbled poetry or did other small household tasks. This left the Mole with a good deal of spare time on his hands. One afternoon while the Rat dozed in his armchair before the fire, the Mole decided to go out by himself and explore the Wild Wood— and perhaps stop by and meet Mr. Badger. Since it was winter, the Badger should be home.

It was a cold afternoon when the Mole slipped out of the warm parlor into the open air. He scampered toward the Wild Wood.

At first, there was nothing to alarm him. Twigs snapped. Logs tripped him. But this was rather fun and exciting. Soon, however, all became very still. The trees seemed to close in on him. The sun began to set, draining away like floodwater.

Then the faces began.

He saw a little, evil, wedge-shaped face looking out from a hole—then it vanished!

Mole quickened his pace, telling himself he was imagining things. But from every hole, far and near, hundreds of faces with hard eyes popped out—flashing, then disappearing!

Becoming fearful, he swung off the path and plunged into the darkening woods.

Then the whistling began.

It was behind him! He hurried forward. Then, he heard whistling ahead of him. He paused, not knowing which way to go. Then the whistling rose up on both sides. He was alone, and unarmed, and far from any help. The night was closing in.

Then the pattering began.

He thought it was only falling leaves at first. But it grew into a pat-pat-pat of little feet. A rabbit came running toward him through the trees. "Get out of this, you fool, get out!" the Mole heard the rabbit mutter as he disappeared down into a burrow.

The pattering increased. In panic, Mole began to run. At last he ducked into a dark hollow of an old beech tree, hiding from the Terror of the Wild Wood.

Meantime, the Rat dozed by the fireside until a coal slipped and he woke with a jump.

"Moly!" he called. There was no answer.

The Rat got up and went into the hall. The Mole's cap was missing from its peg, and his boots were gone. The Rat left the house and looked over the muddy ground outside. There were the Mole's bootprints leading right to the Wild Wood.

Without hesitation, the Rat went back in, strapped a belt around his waist, shoved on a pair of pistols, picked up a thick club, and set off for the Wild Wood at a rapid pace.

He hunted through the Wood for an hour or more calling out cheerfully, "Moly! It's old Rat!" At last, to his joy, he heard a little answering cry. Guiding himself by the sound, he made his way to the foot of an old beech tree and from out of the hole at its base came a feeble voice saying, "Ratty! Is that really you?"

The Rat crept into the hollow of the tree.

"Rat!" cried the Mole. "I've been so frightened!"

"You shouldn't have come here, Mole," said the Rat, with a warm laugh. "We River Bankers, we hardly ever come here by ourselves."

The Mole was cheered by the Rat's laughter.

"We really must start for home," said the Rat.

"Dear Ratty," said the poor Mole, "I'm simply worn out with fear. You *must* let me rest here a while longer."

"Oh, all right," said the Rat. "Have at it."

So the Mole dropped off to sleep.

When at last the Mole awoke, the Rat looked out the hole and said quietly, "Oh, bother!"

"What's up?" asked the Mole.

"*Snow* is up," replied the Rat. Everything had been covered in white. "The worst of it is, I don't exactly know where we are. And now this snow makes everything look so different. We'll just have to do our best as we try to get back home."

An hour or two later—they had lost all track of time—they stopped and sat down on a fallen log. They were cold and wet, tired and aching, and bruised from falling down. There seemed to be no end to this Wild Wood—and no beginning.

"There's a sort of valley down here," said the Rat. "We'll make our way down into that and find some sort of shelter out of the snow and wind."

Once more they got on their feet and struggled down into the valley in the moonlight. Suddenly the Mole tripped and fell forward on his face.

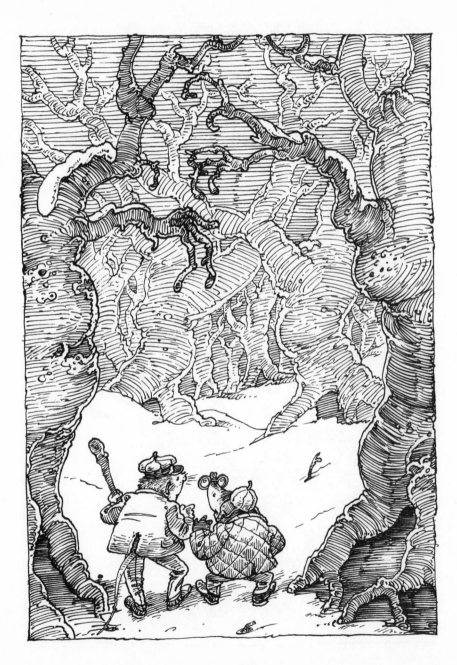

"Oh, my leg!" he cried.

"Let's have a look," said the Rat kindly. "My! You've cut your shin." He wrapped the cut.

"I must have tripped over a stump!"

"No. It's too clean a cut," said the Rat, thinking. "I wonder…" Then the Rat started digging and scratching and soon cried "Hooray!"

"What *have* you found?" asked the Mole.

"Come and see!" said the delighted Rat.

The Mole hobbled up to the spot.

"Well," the Mole said slowly. "A boot scraper! Why get excited over something you scrape your boots on?"

"You dull-witted animal!" the Rat said, and began digging again. In a few moments he had uncovered a very shabby doormat.

"There! What does *that* tell you, you thickheaded beast?" exclaimed the Rat.

"Nothing whatever, you maddening rodent."

"Do—you—mean—to—say," cried the excited Rat, "that this doormat doesn't *tell* you anything? Now look here, you! Scrape and scratch and dig and hunt round, especially if you want to sleep dry and warm tonight!"

The Rat started digging with fury. The Mole followed, but mostly because he thought his friend had gone snow-crazy.

After some ten minutes' hard work, the Rat felt his club strike something that sounded hollow. In the side of a snowbank stood a solid-looking little door. Below the bell-pull was a neatly engraved brass plate that read:

MR. BADGER

The Mole fell backward on the snow. "Rat!" he cried. "You found the boot scraper! And then you found the doormat. Then the door! All because you thought it through!"

"I suppose you're going to sit on the snow all night and *talk*?" interrupted the Rat. "Pull on that bell-pull as I knock!"

While the Rat attacked the door with his club, the Mole sprang up at the bell-pull. And from quite a long way off they could faintly hear a deep-toned doorbell.

CHAPTER FOUR

Badger's Home

They waited patiently for what seemed a very long time. At last the door opened a few inches.

"Who is it *this* time?" asked a gruff voice.

"Oh, Badger," cried the Rat. "It's me, Rat, and my friend Mole. We've lost our way in the snow."

"Lost in the snow!" exclaimed the Badger, in a quite different voice. "And in the Wild Wood, too! But come in with you."

The two animals tumbled over each other to get inside.

The Badger, who wore a long bathrobe, carried a flat candlestick in his paw. He looked kindly down on them and patted both their heads

and said, "This is not the sort of night for small animals to be out."

He shuffled on in front of them, carrying the light. At once they found themselves in all the glow and warmth of a large fire-lit kitchen. It was a cheerful room, just right for friendly chats.

The kindly Badger removed their wet coats and boots and thrust them down on a bench to toast themselves at the fire. Then he fetched them bathrobes and slippers and he himself cleaned and bandaged the Mole's shin till the whole thing was just as good as new, if not better.

When at last they were nicely warmed, the Badger summoned them to the table where he had been busy preparing a meal. For a long time there was no conversation, for the two animals were *so* hungry. When they finally *did* start talking, it was that awful sort of talking with one's mouth full. The Badger did not mind that sort of thing at all. Nor did he notice elbows on the table, or everybody speaking at once. As he did not go into Society himself, Badger didn't believe that these things mattered. (We know of course that he was wrong, because they do matter very much, but it would take too long here to explain why.)

When supper was finished, they gathered round the fire and the Badger said heartily, "Tell us, how's old Toad going on?"

"From bad to worse," said the Rat gravely. "Another smash-up last week. He thinks he's a heaven-born driver!"

"How many does that make?" inquired the Badger gloomily.

"This is the seventh," answered the Rat.

"He's been in the hospital three times," put in the Mole. "And as for the fines he's had to pay, it's simply awful."

"He's going to end up either dead or bankrupt," continued the Rat. "We're his friends—oughtn't we to do something?"

The Badger thought for a moment and then said, "Once spring is here, we'll take Toad seriously in hand. We'll bring him back to reason. We'll *make* him be a sensible Toad. We'll—you're asleep, Rat!"

"Not me!" said the Rat, waking up with a jerk.

"It's time we were all in bed," said the Badger. "Come along and I'll show you your beds. Breakfast at any hour you please."

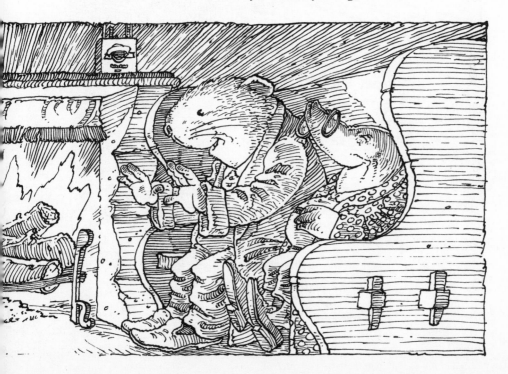

The next morning, the two tired animals came down to breakfast very late and found two young hedgehogs sitting at the table eating oatmeal.

"Where have you youngsters come from?" asked the Rat pleasantly. "Lost your way in the snow, I suppose?"

"Yes, sir," said the older hedgehog. "We were trying to find our way to school—Mother *would* have us go regardless of the weather—and we lost ourselves, and at last we happened up against Mr. Badger's back door—"

"I understand," said the Rat, cutting himself some bacon while the Mole fried eggs. "What's the weather like?"

"Terrible deep the snow is, sir," said the hedgehog. "And Mr. Badger's gone into his study. He said he had a lot of work to do this particular morning, so he was not to be disturbed."

The Rat winked at the Mole. The animals knew that Badger, having eaten a hearty breakfast, had retired to his study for a winter's nap.

The frontdoor bell clanged loudly and the Rat sent the smaller hedgehog to see who it might be. The hedgehog returned with the Otter.

"Thought I would find you here," said the Otter cheerfully. "No one at home at your place. Everyone said something bad had happened. I didn't believe it. Thought Moly had probably let his curiosity get the best of him. He's talked about Badger all summer. Just to be sure, though, I came straight here. Badger's the chap, eh?" he laughed. "Here, Mole, fry me some ham. Must speak to Ratty here. Haven't seen him since yesterday."

The Mole had the hedgehogs fry some ham and he returned to his own breakfast. The Otter and the Rat eagerly talked River Bank gossip.

A plate of fried ham had just been cleared and sent back for more when the Badger entered and greeted them all. "It must be getting lunchtime," he remarked to the Otter. "You must be hungry this cold morning."

"Rather!" replied the Otter, winking at the Mole. "The sight of these greedy young hedgehogs eating all the ham makes me feel positively starved."

The hedgehogs, who *were* beginning to feel hungry again after working so hard at their frying, looked timidly up at Mr. Badger, but were too shy to correct the Otter's fib.

"You two youngsters be off home to your mother," said the Badger kindly. "You won't want any lunch today, I'll say. Goodness! What you must have already eaten."

After the hedgehogs had left, they all sat down to lunch together. The Mole found himself placed next to Mr. Badger. He told him how comfortable and homelike Badger's place felt to him.

The Badger grinned. "I agree! There's no security, or peace, or quiet except underground. And, above all, no *weather*. Look at Rat, now. A couple of feet of floodwater and he's got to move out and rent a place. Uncomfortable, a bother, and horribly expensive. Take Toad. I say nothing against Toad Hall—quite the best house in these parts, *as* a house. But supposing a fire breaks out—where's Toad? Supposing roof tiles are blown off, or walls sink or crack, or windows get broken—where's Toad? Supposing the rooms are drafty—I *hate* a draft myself—where's Toad? Underground—that's my idea of *home*."

The Mole nodded enthusiastically and the Badger felt friendly toward him. "When lunch is over," he said, "I'll take you round this little place of mine. I can see you'll appreciate it."

After lunch, the Badger did just that. The Mole was amazed at all the passageways and huge rooms with pillars and archways. "It used to be part of a city made by people long ago," explained the Badger. "They thought it would last forever… but now it is part of the Wild Wood. The people are gone, and the animals are here—both good and bad. It takes all sorts to make a world."

"I've met some…" said the Mole with a shiver.

"Well, well," said the Badger. "We must live and let live. I'll pass the word that you're my friend. You'll have no more trouble in the Wild Wood."

After Mole had finished with his tour and returned to the kitchen, the Rat said, "Come along, Mole. We don't want to spend another night in the Wild Wood."

"You really needn't fret, Ratty," stated the Badger calmly. "When you really have to go, you shall leave by one of my shortcuts."

The Rat was still anxious to be off and attend to his river, so the Badger led the way along a damp tunnel that seemed to go on for miles. At last, daylight began to show itself through a vine-covered hole. The Badger wished them well and waved good-bye.

As the three emerged from the tunnel on the edge of the Wild Wood, the Otter took charge and they followed behind him in a beeline. Pausing for a moment, though, they looked back at the Wild Wood, dark and thick and scary. Then, they happily turned and made swiftly for home.

They traveled quietly, each thinking his own private thoughts. Mole saw his life clearly. He was an animal of field and hedgerow. He knew he belonged with pleasant pastures and quiet country lanes and well-tended garden plots. Others could have the harshness of the Wild Wood, the hard life, roughing it with Nature. He had dared to venture forth—and he had found his place. He hurried on, content and at peace.

CHAPTER FIVE

Home Sweet Home

The Rat and the Mole were returning to the River Bank one day after a long outing with Otter. The shades of the short winter day were closing in on them. On either side of the road they could smell the friendly fields through the darkness. They still had some distance to go till the rattle of the door latch, the sudden firelight, and the sight of familiar things would greet them. They plodded silently. The Mole was thinking about supper. The Rat was walking a little way ahead, his eyes fixed on the road in front. He did not notice poor Mole when the "silent voice" suddenly reached Mole and shook him like an electric shock.

His nose searched hither and thither.

Home! He smelled it! Since his escape on that bright morning when he'd given up spring-cleaning and had gone to live on the river with Rat, he had hardly given his old home a thought. Now, with a rush of old memories, how clearly it stood up before him in the darkness.

"Ratty!" Mole called, full of joyful excitement. "Hold on! I want you, quick!"

"Oh, *come* along, Mole!" replied the Rat cheerfully, still plodding along.

"*Please* stop, Ratty!" pleaded the poor Mole. "You don't understand! It's my old home! I've just come across the smell of it. I *must* go to it!"

The Rat was by this time very far ahead, too far to clearly hear what the Mole was calling. "We mustn't stop now!" he called back. "The snow's coming on again! I need your nose, Mole, so come quick!"

Poor Mole stood alone in the road, his heart torn into pieces. But never for a moment did he dream of abandoning his friend. With an effort, he caught up to the Rat, who began chattering cheerfully, never noticing the Mole's silence. At last, however, the Rat stopped and said kindly,

"Mole, you seem dead tired. No talk left in you, and your feet dragging like lead. We'll sit down here for a minute and rest. The snow has held off so far."

The Mole dropped hopelessly on a tree stump and tried to control himself, fighting off a sob. But poor Mole finally gave up the struggle and cried.

The Rat did not dare to speak for a while. At last he said, "What is it, old fellow?"

Poor Mole found it difficult to get any words out. "I know it's a—dingy little place—not like—your cozy home—or Toad's beautiful hall—or Badger's great house—but it was my own little home—and I went away and forgot about it—and then I smelt it—and you wouldn't listen—and—"

The Rat sat and stared straight ahead, saying nothing. After Mole's sobbing grew quieter, the Rat rose from his seat and set off up the road.

"Wherever are you going?" cried the tearful Mole. "You're going the wrong way."

"Follow me."

"Think of River Bank, and your supper!"

"Hang River Bank, and supper too!" said the Rat heartily. "Let's find your home."

They moved on in silence till suddenly Mole stood still for a moment, and then began to run.

The Rat, much excited, kept close to his heels. The Mole scrambled through a hedge, and with no warning, dived into a tunnel. The Rat promptly followed him.

It seemed a long time to Rat before the passage ended and he could stand up straight. The Mole lit a hanging lamp. By its light the Rat saw that they were standing in an open space, neatly swept and sanded underfoot. Directly facing them was Mole's little front door with "Mole End" painted over the doorbell.

Mole's face beamed with excitement and he hurried Rat through the door—into the lonely, empty, neglected house. Mole's face dropped.

"Oh, Ratty!" he cried. "Why did I bring you to this poor, cold little place when you might have been at River Bank, toasting your toes, with all your own nice things about you?"

The Rat paid no heed to Mole's self-pity. "What an excellent little house this is!" he called out cheerily. "We'll make a jolly night of it. I'll fetch the wood and you get a dust cloth and try and smarten things up a bit!"

Mole dusted while the Rat, running to and fro, soon had a blaze roaring up the chimney. Mole promptly had another fit of the blues. "Rat," he moaned, "how about your supper? I've nothing to give you—not a crumb!"

"I saw a sardine-tin opener," said the Rat. "Everybody knows that means there are sardines about somewhere." Soon Rat had found a tin of sardines and a box of crackers. "There's a banquet for you!" observed the Rat.

Before the Rat could open the sardines, they heard sounds coming from the courtyard outside.

"What's up?" inquired the Rat.

"I think it must be the field mice," replied the Mole with a touch of pride. "They go round carol-singing at this time of the year. And they never pass me over. I used to give them hot drinks, and supper too sometimes, when I could afford it."

"Let's have a look at them!" cried the Rat.

It was a pretty sight, and a festive one, that met their eyes. In the courtyard, lit by the dim rays of a lantern, eight little field mice stood in a semicircle, with red woolen scarves round their throats, their forepaws thrust deep into their pockets, their feet jigging for warmth.

As the door opened, one of the elder ones was just saying, "Now then, one, two, three!" and then their shrill little voices rose up into the air.

CAROL

Here we stand in the cold and the sleet,
Blowing fingers and stamping feet,
Come from far away you to greet—
You by the fire and we in the street—
 Bidding you joy in the morning!

Goodman Joseph toiled through the snow—
Saw the star o'er a stable low.
Mary she might not further go—
Welcome roof, and straw below!
 Joy was hers in the morning!

And then they heard the angels tell,
"Who were the first to cry Noel?
Animals all, as it befell,
In the stable where they did dwell!
 Joy shall be theirs in the morning!"

"Very well sung!" cried the Rat heartily. "And now come along in, all of you, and have something hot!"

"We've nothing to give them!" cried Mole in despair. "Only sardines!"

"You leave that to me," said the masterful Rat. "You with the lantern! I want to talk to you."

There was whispering, the field mouse was given money and a basket, and off he hurried.

The rest of the field mice, perched in a row on a comfy bench with their small legs swinging, enjoyed the fire. They toasted their frozen toes till they tingled.

It did not take long for Rat to prepare warm spiced tea. Soon every field mouse was sipping (for a little spiced tea goes a long way) and laughing and forgetting he had ever been cold in all his life. Time passed quickly and all at once the latch clicked, the door opened, and the field mouse with the lantern came in, staggering under the weight of his basket.

In a very few minutes supper was ready. Mole took the head place and looked at the table now overflowing with food. He saw his little friends' faces brighten and beam as they began eating. He thought what a happy homecoming this had become. The Rat said little, only taking care that each guest had what he wanted, and plenty of it.

That night, the weary Mole was glad to turn in. But before he closed his eyes, he let them wander round his old room. He saw how plain and simple it all was, but also how much it all meant. He did not want to abandon the new life. The upper world was all too strong. It called to him. But it was good to think he had this to come back to, this place that was all his own, these things that could always be counted upon for the same simple welcome.

The River was his adventure.

This was home.

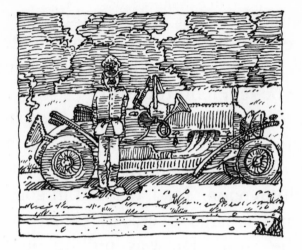

CHAPTER SIX

Mr. Toad

It was a bright morning in the early part of summer. The Mole and the Water Rat were just finishing breakfast when a heavy knock sounded at the door. The Mole went to answer and the Rat heard him utter a cry of surprise. "Mr. Badger!"

The Badger strode heavily into the room.

"The hour has come!" said the Badger.

"What hour?" asked the Rat.

"*Whose* hour, you should rather ask," replied the Badger. "The hour of Toad! I'm going to straighten out his miserable life today!"

"Toad's hour! Hooray! *We'll* teach him to be a sensible Toad!" cried the Mole.

"A new motorcar is being delivered today," continued the Badger. "At this moment, Toad is busy dressing himself in that awful driving outfit. He *must* be taken off the road."

They set off immediately and reached Toad Hall to find, as the Badger had said, a shiny new motorcar in front of the house. The door of the house flung open. Toad, dressed in goggles, cap, boots, and a large overcoat, came swaggering down the steps. He was pulling on his long driving gloves.

"Hullo!" Toad cried cheerfully. "You're just in time to come for a jolly—to come for a—er—" Toad noticed the stern looks of his silent friends.

Badger walked up the steps. "Take him inside," he said to his companions. As the struggling Toad was hustled through the door, Badger told the waiting driver, "Mr. Toad has changed his mind. He will not require the car." Then Badger followed the others inside.

Toad's ridiculous motor-clothes were promptly removed while Toad kicked and called out names. Finally, there he stood—merely Toad again, no longer the Terror of the Highway. Toad giggled feebly and looked from one to the other.

"You knew it must come to this sooner or later, Toad," the Badger said. "You don't listen to our warnings. You've gone on wasting the money your father left you. You're giving us animals a bad name by your breakneck driving, your smashes, and your run-ins with the police. You will come with me into the library and we'll talk this out."

He took Toad firmly by the arm, led him into the library, and closed the door behind them.

"*That's* no good!" said the Rat. "*Talking* to Toad will never cure him. He'll *say* anything."

After forty-five minutes the door opened.

"Toad has seen the folly of his ways," said the smiling Badger. "Haven't you, Toad?"

There was a long, long pause.

"No!" Toad said. "I *haven't*. It's not folly—it's simply glorious!"

"What?" cried the Badger. "Didn't you tell me just now, in there—"

"Oh yes, in *there*," said Toad. "I'd have said anything in *there*."

"Then you don't promise," said the Badger, "never to touch a motorcar again?"

"Certainly not!" replied Toad. "I promise that the first motorcar I see, toot-toot! off I go in it!"

"Then we'll try force," said the Badger. "Lock him in his bedroom."

"It's for your own good," said the Rat kindly as they hauled kicking, struggling Toad up the stairs.

"We'll take great care of everything for you till you're well, Toad," said the Mole, "and we'll see your money isn't wasted, as it has been."

"No more run-ins with the police," said the Rat.

"And no more hospital stays," added the Mole as they locked Toad inside.

They went back down the stairs with Toad shouting at them through the keyhole.

"It's going to be a long ordeal," said the Badger, sighing.

They took turns standing watch, taking care to never let Toad out of sight, or out of his room. At first Toad threw temper tantrums and was very difficult for his guardians. He would arrange his bedroom chairs as a "motorcar" and get in—bent forward into the wind—making ghastly engine noises until even his makeshift car toppled over as he flipped through the air. There he would lie on the floor with a smile on his face. As time went on, however, he had fewer fits, and he became more quiet, droopy, and depressed.

One morning, Rat, whose turn it was to go on duty, went upstairs to relieve Badger.

"Toad's still in bed," Badger told the Rat, outside the door. "You be careful, Rat! When Toad is quiet, he's at his trickiest. I must be off."

"How are you today?" inquired the Rat as he approached Toad's bedside.

At last Toad feebly murmured, "Thank you for asking. But tell me about yourself and Mole."

"Mole has gone with Badger until lunchtime."

The Rat did not see Toad's eyes as they twinkled slightly.

"You're tired of bothering about me," sighed Toad. "I'm a nuisance, I know."

"You are, indeed," said the Rat. "But I'd take any trouble on earth for you if only you'd be a sensible animal."

"Then I would beg you," said Toad even more feebly, "—even though it may be too late— to step round the village and fetch the doctor."

"Why do you want a doctor?"

"Never mind—forget I asked," said Toad weakly.

"Look here," said the Rat, beginning to get rather alarmed, "of course I'll fetch a doctor if you really think you want him."

"Would you mind at the same time asking the lawyer to step up?" asked Toad.

"A lawyer! Oh, he must be really bad!" the frightened Rat said to himself as he hurried from the room. He did not forget, however, to lock the door carefully behind him.

"I've known Toad to ask for a doctor before," Rat said to himself, "but I've never heard him ask for a lawyer! I wish Badger and Mole were here. Oh, it's best to be on the safe side." So he ran off to the village.

Toad watched Rat disappear down the drive. Then, laughing heartily, he dressed and filled his pockets with cash from the dresser. Next, he knotted the sheets from his bed together into a rope, and scrambled out the bedroom window.

At first Toad took back roads, crossed many fields, and changed his course several times in case he was followed. But now, feeling safe, with the sun smiling brightly on him, he danced along the road in his satisfaction and conceit.

"Smart piece of work!" chuckled Toad. He held his head in the air, full of self-praise, till he reached a little town where he saw a sign:

THE RED LION INN

This reminded him he had not eaten that day. He marched into the Inn and ordered lunch.

He was about halfway through his meal when a familiar sound coming down the street made him tremble. The toot-toot! drew nearer and Toad heard the car turn into the Inn yard. Then the passengers, chatting and giggling about their drive, entered the room. Toad listened until he could stand it no longer. He paid and slipped out to the Inn yard. "There cannot be any harm," he said to himself, "in my only just looking at it!"

And there the car stood in the middle of the yard quite unattended. "I wonder," he said to himself, "if this sort of car starts easily?"

As if in a dream, Toad found himself, somehow, seated in the driver's seat. As if in a dream, he pulled the starting lever and swung the car out onto the roadway. He increased his speed! As the car devoured the street and leaped down the highroad through the open country, he was only aware that he was TOAD once more. Toad at his best and highest. Toad the Terror, the traffic-stopper, the lord of the lone trail before whom all must give way or be knocked into everlasting night. It didn't occur to him that he'd just stolen a car...

"Mr. Clerk," observed the Judge, "will you tell us the stiffest penalty we can impose?"

The Clerk scratched his nose with his pen and looked at Toad. "I'd say twelve months for the theft, three years for the furious driving, and fifteen years for being rude to the police—those figures, if added together, tot up to nineteen years—I'd make it an even twenty."

"An excellent suggestion!" said the Judge. "Prisoner! It's going to be twenty years for you this time. Take him away!"

Then the brutal assistants of the law fell upon the unlucky Toad. They loaded him with chains, and dragged him from the Court House, shrieking, praying, protesting—across the marketplace, and into the deepest, darkest dungeon of the best-guarded jail of the strongest castle in all the length and breadth of Merry England.

CHAPTER SEVEN

The Protector of Small Creatures

It was after ten o'clock at night and Mole lay stretched on the riverbank, still panting from the heat of the day. He heard the Rat's light footfall and, sure enough, Rat plopped down next to him.

"You stayed late at Otter's," said Mole.

"I'm afraid the Otters are in trouble," said the Rat. "Little Portly is missing again."

"He's always straying off," said the Mole lightly, "but no harm happens. We've found him ourselves, miles from home!"

"This time it's more serious," said the Rat. "He's been missing for some days now. The Otters have hunted everywhere. They've asked every animal, too, for miles around. Otter's more worried than he'll admit. He is going to spend the night watching by the shallow area where he gave Portly his first swimming lesson. It was there he used to teach him fishing, and there young Portly caught his first fish. The child loved the spot and Otter thinks that if he wanders back from wherever he is that he might stop there and play, perhaps. So Otter goes there every night and watches."

"Rat," said the Mole, "if this is serious, I simply can't go and turn in, and go to sleep, and do nothing, even though there doesn't seem to be anything to be done. We'll get the boat out and paddle upstream. The moon will be up soon. We'll take a look around."

"Just what I was thinking myself," said the Rat. "Daybreak is not far off, and we may pick up some news from early risers as we go along."

They got the boat out and worked their way up the stream. All night they searched. The dark was filled with small noises, songs, and chattering. They explored hedges and ditches and tunnels. The moon, serene and alone in a cloudless sky, did what she could, till her hour came and she sank toward the earth, and left them.

The Rat sat up suddenly and listened to a breeze. Mole looked at him with curiosity.

"It's gone!" sighed the Rat, sinking back in his seat again. "No! There it is again!" Entranced, he was silent for a long space.

"I hear nothing myself," the Mole said, "but the wind playing in the willows."

In silence, Mole rowed steadily, and soon they came to where the river divided. In the middle of one side was a small, flowered island.

"Now you must surely hear it!" cried the Rat joyously. "Ah—at last—I see you do!"

Breathless and transfixed, the Mole stopped rowing. No birds sang. A heavenly melody floated through the fresh dawn air. All the colors were brighter. All was peaceful, still, and lovely.

Slowly the two animals landed at the island, and pushed through the blossoms and hedges that led to a little level lawn with fruit trees.

"This is the place of my song dream," said Rat.

Mole felt a great Awe fall upon him—not from panic but from wonder and peace. He lowered his head. Something noble was very near.

The music stopped. Trembling, Mole raised his humble head and looked up—into the very eyes of the Friend and Helper, the Protector of Small Creatures. He saw the curved horns, the stern, hooked nose between the kindly eyes, the bearded mouth broken into a smile. He saw the rippling muscles on the arm that lay across the broad chest, and the hand holding the reed Pan-pipes. He saw the splendid curves of the shaggy limbs on the grass and saw, nestling between his very hooves, sleeping soundly in peace and contentment, the little, round, pudgy, childish form of the baby otter.

"Rat!" Mole found breath to whisper, unsure if the Rat saw what he saw. "Are you afraid?"

"Afraid?" murmured the Rat. "Oh, never! And yet—I am afraid!"

Then the two animals bowed their heads humbly. When they looked once more, the Vision had vanished and the air was full of the carol of birds.

As they stared blankly, a whimsical little breeze brought instant forgetfulness. For this is the last gift that the kindly Protector of Small Creatures gives those to whom he has revealed himself. If forgetfulness were not given, daily life could no longer offer happiness against the memory of such an experience.

Mole rubbed his eyes and stared at Rat, who was looking about him in a puzzled sort of way. "What did you say, Rat?" he asked.

"I was only remarking," said Rat slowly, "that—why, there he is!"

Portly woke up with a joyous squeak at the sight of his father's friends. Then, looking for something he couldn't find or see, he finally sat down and cried.

The Mole ran quickly to comfort the little animal, but Rat looked long and doubtfully at certain hoof-marks deep in the soft grass.

"Some—great—animal—has been here," he murmured slowly and thoughtfully.

"Come along, Rat!" called the Mole. "Think of poor Otter, waiting up there by the shallow area!"

The two animals loaded Portly into the boat, and paddled down the river.

As they drew near the shallow area, the Mole lifted Portly out. They watched the little animal as he waddled along the path happily. Looking up the river, they could see Otter, tense and rigid, and could hear his amazed and joyous bark as he bounded up through the willows toward his long-lost son.

"I feel as if I had been through something very exciting and rather awesome," said the Mole, "and it was just over, and yet nothing particular has happened."

"Isn't it jolly to feel the sun again soaking into one's bones!" sighed the Rat, leaning back and closing his eyes. "And listen to the wind playing in the reeds!"

"It's like music," said the Mole drowsily.

"Dance music," murmured the Rat. "The lilting sort that runs nonstop—but with words in it."

"You hear better than I," said the Mole sadly. "I cannot catch the words."

"Let me try and give you them," said the Rat.

> *Lest the awe should dwell—*
> *And turn your frolic to fret—*
> *   You shall look on my power*
> *   At the helping hour—*
> *But then you shall forget!*

"But what do the words mean?" asked the wondering Mole.

But no answer came. The weary Rat was fast asleep.

CHAPTER EIGHT

Toad's Adventures

When Toad found himself in prison, he flung himself on the floor and shed bitter tears.

"This is the end," he howled. "O unhappy and forsaken Toad!" With cries such as these he passed his days and nights for several weeks, refusing even food and drink.

Now, the jailer had a daughter who helped her father in the lighter duties of his job. She was quite fond of animals and said to her father one day, "Father! I can't bear to see that poor beast so unhappy and getting so thin! Let me take care of him. You know how I like animals. I'll make him eat from my hand, sit up, and do all sorts of things."

Her father agreed. So that day she went on her errand of mercy and knocked at the door of Toad's cell.

"Now, cheer up, Toad," she said, on entering. "Sit up and be a sensible animal. And do try and eat a bit of dinner."

Toad sat up slowly, dried his eyes, sipped some tea, munched some toast, and soon began talking freely about himself, the house he lived in, his doings there, and how important he was.

The jailer's daughter saw that the topic was helping Toad as much as the tea.

"Tell me about Toad Hall," said she.

"Toad Hall," said the Toad proudly, "is a gentleman's residence dating in part from the fourteenth century, but complete with every modern convenience. Up-to-date plumbing. Five minutes from church, post office, golf courses—"

"I don't want to *buy* it," said the girl, laughing. "Tell me something *real* about it."

Toad then told her more about Toad Hall and stories of him at his best: singing songs, telling stories, entertaining. When she said goodnight, Toad was very much the same self-satisfied, confident animal that he had been of old.

They had many interesting talks together after that. The jailer's daughter felt Toad had been wrongly imprisoned for a one-car wreck and for being rude. Toad, of course, in his vanity, thought she had fallen in love with him and felt it sad that he would have to break her heart.

One morning, the girl did not seem to be paying proper attention to Toad's sparkling comments and witty sayings. "Toad," she interrupted, "just listen, please. I have an aunt who is a washerwoman."

"Think no more about it," said Toad, "*I* have several aunts who *ought* to be washerwomen."

"Do be quiet, Toad," said the girl. "You talk too much. As I said, I have an aunt who is a washerwoman. She does the washing for all the prisoners in this castle. I think if she were approached in the right way—bribed, I believe is the word—she would let you have her dress and bonnet, and you could escape from the castle as a washerwoman. You two have the same figure."

"We *don't*," said the Toad in a huff. "I have a very elegant figure—for what I am."

"So has my aunt," replied the girl, "for what *she* is. Being Mr. Toad of Toad Hall, I suppose you wish to be escorted from prison in a carriage!"

Toad knew she was right. If he wanted out of prison, he must be humble—at least for a moment.

"Introduce me to your aunt," he said. "We'll make a deal."

Next evening, the girl ushered her aunt into Toad's cell. The sight of certain gold coins that Toad had placed on the table in full view convinced the aunt. In return for his cash, Toad received a cotton gown, an apron, a shawl, and a faded black bonnet.

"You're the very image of her," the jailer's daughter giggled. "Now, good-bye, dear Toad, and good luck."

With a quaking heart, but firm footsteps, Toad set forth cautiously on what seemed to be a most harebrained and dangerous task. But he was soon surprised at how easily he passed for the washerwoman. Prison guards let him pass through every gate and door he came to. They also called out silly remarks and flirted with the "washerwoman." Toad managed to hold his tongue, but he *was* quite offended, indeed.

It seemed hours before he crossed the last courtyard, but at last he heard the iron gate click behind him, and knew that he was free!

Some red and green lights and the sound of a train engine caught his attention. He made his way to the railway station and found that a train, bound in the direction of his home, was due to start in half an hour. "More luck!" said Toad as he went to the booking office to buy his ticket.

He gave the name of the station in the village near Toad Hall and put his fingers, in search of the money, where his vest pocket should have been. He fumbled all through the dress and found—not only no money, but *no pocket*, and *no vest* to hold a pocket! To his horror he remembered he had left both coat and vest behind in his cell, along with his wallet, money, keys, watch, matches, pencil case—all that makes life worth living.

The clerk stared at him and the faded black bonnet a moment, and laughed. "Either pay or move, madam. You're blocking other passengers!"

Baffled and full of despair, Toad wandered blindly down the station platform where the train was standing, and tears trickled down each side of his nose.

"Hullo, little mother!" said the engine driver. "What's the trouble?"

"I am a poor washerwoman!" said Toad, crying. "I've lost all my money, and I must get home tonight somehow!"

"Got some kids, too, waiting for you?" asked the engine driver.

"And they'll be hungry," sobbed Toad, "and playing with matches!"

"If you'll wash a few shirts for me when you get home," said the good engine driver, "I'll give you a ride. It's against rules, but no one will know."

Toad scrambled up into the cab, agreeing to something he had no intention of doing.

They covered many and many a mile. Toad was already thinking of what to have for supper as soon as he got home, when he noticed that the engine driver was leaning over the side of the train and listening hard. "It's very strange," he said to Toad. "We're the last train running in this direction tonight, yet there's an engine on our rails coming along at a great pace! With men waving axes, Billy-clubs, revolvers, and canes. All shouting the same thing—'Stop, stop, stop!' "

Then Toad fell on his knees and cried, "I will confess all! I'm not a simple washerwoman! I am the well-known and popular Mr. Toad, the squire of Toad Hall. I have just escaped from prison. Please, sir, don't make me go back! Help me!"

The engine driver looked down upon him very sternly. "What were you put in prison for?"

"I only *borrowed* a motorcar," answered Toad. "I didn't mean to *steal* it."

"I don't like motorcars," said the driver. "Steal them all, if you want. Cheer up, Toad! I'll do my best, and we may beat them yet!"

They tried to outrun them, but their pursuers slowly gained. The engine driver said, "There's just one thing left to do. Up ahead is a tunnel, followed by some woods. We'll rush through the tunnel. When we are through, I will shut off the steam and put on the brakes, and the moment it's safe you must jump and hide in the woods before they get through the tunnel and see you."

They piled on more coals and the train shot into the tunnel and out the other side. The driver shut off the steam and put on the brakes, and as the train slowed down Toad heard the driver call out, "Now, jump!"

Toad jumped, rolled down a short hill, picked himself up unhurt, and scrambled into the safety of the woods.

Peeping out, he saw his train disappear at a great pace. Then out of the tunnel burst the pursuing engine. When they were past and the woods became silent, Toad had a hearty laugh.

But he soon stopped laughing. It was now very late and dark and cold, and he was in unknown woods with no money, no chance of supper, and still far from friends and home. Finding a hollow tree, he crawled inside, and did his best to sleep.

CHAPTER NINE

Wanderers All

The Water Rat was restless, and he did not exactly know why. There was a feeling in the air of change and departure.

Leaving the waterside, Rat wandered toward the country. He crossed a few meadows and pastures, and thrust into a field of ripened wheat. Here Rat had many friends who were always up for gossip. Today, however, the field mice and harvest mice seemed busy. Many were digging and tunneling. Some were hauling out dusty suitcases, others were packing their belongings, while everywhere piles of grain lay bundled and ready to be moved.

"You know it isn't time to be thinking of winter quarters yet!" said the Water Rat sternly.

"Oh, yes, we know that," explained a field mouse, "but we really *must* get all the furniture moved out of this field before those horrid harvesting machines begin clicking round the wheat. We're only just making a start."

"Oh, bother *starts*," said the Rat. "It's a splendid day. Come for a row on the river, or a stroll along the hedges, or a picnic in the woods—or something."

"Well, I *think* not *today*," replied the field mouse hurriedly. "Perhaps some *other* day—when we've more *time*—"

The Rat, with a snort, swung round to go, and returned somewhat grumpily to his river again.

In the willows that lined the River Bank he overheard several swallows talking together about their upcoming travels to the South.

"What's the hurry?" asked the Rat.

"Oh, we're not off *yet*," replied the first swallow. "We're only making plans and arranging things. Talking it over—what route we're taking this year, where we'll stop, and so on. That's half the fun!"

"Fun?" asked the Rat. "I don't know what's fun about leaving your home."

"No, you don't understand," said the second swallow. "It's natural for us. First, we feel it stirring within us, a sweet unrest. We hunger to talk with each other, to compare notes. It's exciting, this anticipation."

"Couldn't you stay on for just this year?" suggested the Water Rat. "I hate to see everyone go. It gets so lonesome."

"I tried that once," said the third swallow. "But then the cold came. And the insects all disappeared. I was forced to leave. I shall never forget the blissful feeling, after I arrived, of the hot southern sun again on my back, and the taste of my first fat insect! Never again will I *not* go South, said I."

"Ah, yes, the call of the South!" twittered the other two dreamily. "Its songs, its hues, its radiant air! Oh, you remember—"

"But there is also the call to come back," the first swallow interrupted, "in due season. The song of lush meadow grass, wet orchards, warm, insect-haunted ponds, of browsing cattle, of hay-making, and all the farm buildings clustering round the House of the Perfect Eaves."

The Rat wandered off once more, feeling restless. He traveled down the dusty lane until he came to a shady spot. There he lay in the thick, cool underbrush, and dreamed about the paved road and how it must lead to wondrous worlds— places other animals had gone, but never him.

He heard footsteps and a figure came into view. He saw that it was a rat, and a very dusty one, who looked weary. The traveler, with a pleasant smile, turned from the road and sat down by Rat's side under the cool vines and tangles. He was thin, with small, sharp features. His paws were slender and long. His eyes were wrinkled at the corners. He wore small gold earrings in his neatly-shaped ears. He wore a faded blue knitted sweater, and his pants were patched and stained. All he carried was a bundle of things tied up in a blue cotton handkerchief.

"This is a beautiful place," the stranger remarked. "It is a goodly life that you lead, friend, no doubt the best in the world!"

"Yes, it's the *only* life to live," responded the Water Rat.

"I did not say exactly that," replied the stranger. "But no doubt it's the best. I've tried it.

And even though I've tried it—six months of it—I'm leaving it to go South, back to the old life which will not let me go."

"You are not one of us," said the Water Rat. "You're not a farmer, nor even of this country."

"Right," replied the stranger. "I'm a Seafaring Rat. I was born in the port of Constantinople, though I'm a sort of stranger there, too, in a way. My family, all seafaring rats, is from there.

As for me, my home is any pleasant coastal city between here and there. I know them all, and they know me. Set me down on any of their docks or beaches, and I am home again."

"Well, perhaps you have chosen the better way," said the Water Rat. "Tell me something of your sea travels then, if you don't mind. What sort of memories do you bring home to warm your days by the fireside? To tell the truth, I was thinking today that my life is somewhat boring. I'm starting to hate it. Everyone else is leaving. I should be leaving, too."

The Sea Rat began to tell the Water Rat amazing stories of real but strange places. The stories sounded as if they were out of fairy tales, with strange foods and customs—exciting towns and ports and places unknown.

"It must be a hard life," murmured the Rat, not really believing his own words.

"Well, what do *you* think?" asked the Sea Rat with a weary smile and a wink.

"That reminds me," said the polite Water Rat, noting the time. "Would you stay and take lunch with me? My River Bank home is close by."

"Now, I call that kind of you," said the Sea Rat, "and I shall accept your offer. But couldn't you fetch it along out here? I can't stop for long. I've got that ship to catch, you know."

In no time, the Water Rat had fetched the lunch basket and the two animals began to eat.

The Sea Rat continued stories of his travels. Spellbound and quivering with excitement, the Water Rat followed the Adventurer mile-by-mile, over stormy bays, through crowded boathouses, across harbor barriers, over racing tide.

Finally, the Sea Rat rose to his feet. He was still speaking, and still holding the Water Rat's attention with his sea-gray eyes.

"Thanking you for lunch," he said softly, "I take to the road again till at last I reach the sea town I know so well. And you, you will come too, young brother. The days pass and never return, and the South still waits for you. Take the Adventure! Heed the call, before the moment is gone! 'Tis but a banging of the door behind you, a carefree step forward, and you are out of the old life and into the new! Then some day, some day long from now, jog home here if you want when the play has been played, and sit down by your quiet river with your goodly memories for company. You can easily catch up with me on the road, for you are young, and I am aging and go slowly. I will linger and look back. At last I will surely see you coming, eager and lighthearted, with all the South in your face!"

The old Sea Rat's voice died away into silence. The Water Rat sat in a daze. He saw at last but a distant speck on the white surface of the road.

As if in a trance, he rose and repacked the lunch basket. He returned home, gathered up a

few special treasures he was fond of and put them in a bag. He moved about the room like a sleepwalker. He swung the bag over his shoulder on a stout walking stick for his journey. Then, slowly but steadily, he stepped out onto the bank just as the Mole appeared.

"Where are you off to, Ratty?" asked the Mole.

"Going South with the rest of them," murmured the Rat.

The Mole, now much alarmed, stepped in front of the Water Rat, dragged him inside, and placed him in a chair. The Rat mumbled of strange and wild adventures, then sank into a deep slumber.

The Mole left him for a time and busied himself with household matters. It was getting dark when he returned to the parlor. He found the Rat where he had left him, wide-awake indeed, but limp and silent.

The Mole could see that the Rat's strange fit had passed. Rat was now sane again, though he seemed weak and shaken. So the Mole began to talk of other matters. He talked about the important matters of home. He talked about the harvest moon rising that very night over bare acres dotted with grain bundles.

Little by little, the Rat began to sit up and to join in—about the harvest and apples and jams and jellies and their snug home life.

The Mole placed a pencil and a few half-sheets of paper on the table at his friend's elbow.

"It's quite a long time since you did any poetry," Mole remarked.

The Rat pushed the paper away from him, but the understanding Mole left him alone with the paper.

When Mole peeped in again sometime later, the Rat was scribbling away, pausing at times to chew the top of his pencil, in deep thought. It was joy to the Mole to know that the cure had at last begun.

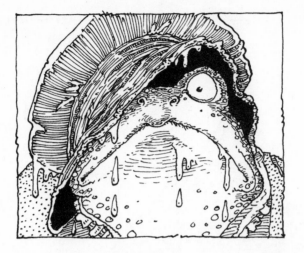

CHAPTER TEN

The Further Adventures of Toad

The front door of the hollow tree faced east. Sitting up, Toad rubbed his eyes first and his toes next. Then he remembered everything—his grand escape, the followers, his leap from the train—and, best of all, his freedom!

He had the world to himself that early summer morning. Toad, however, was looking for something that could talk. Someone who could tell him clearly which way to go to get back to Toad Hall.

He found a road, and the road then found a canal. Toad followed both, marching on patiently by the water's edge.

Soon, Toad noticed a pleasant swirl of quiet water. Then a barge, pulled by a horse, slid up alongside of Toad. The only person on the barge was a big, stout woman wearing a sunbonnet.

"A nice morning, ma'am!" she said to Toad.

"I dare say it is, ma'am!" responded Toad politely as he walked alongside. "A nice morning to anyone who is not in trouble. For me it is but sadness. My married daughter has sent for me. So I've left my washing business at home, where my other children are now alone, tearing the house apart like monkeys. And I've become lost, and my money is gone. If I could only find my way."

"Where might your married daughter be living?" asked the barge woman.

"Close to a fine house called Toad Hall," replied Toad.

"Toad Hall?" asked the barge woman. "This canal joins the river some miles farther on, a little above Toad Hall. You come along in the barge with me."

She steered the barge close to the bank and Toad stepped aboard.

"So you're in the washing business?" asked the barge woman.

"Finest business in the whole country," bragged Toad. "Anyone who's important comes to me. They wouldn't go to anyone else if they were paid. Oh, I have twenty girls who work for me. I love it. Never so happy as when I've got both arms in the washtub."

"What a bit of luck!" said the barge woman.

"What do you mean?" asked Toad nervously.

"I never have time to wash *my* clothes," replied the barge woman. "There's a heap of sweaty clothes in the cabin. You can start by washing my underclothes."

"Here, you let me steer!" said Toad, now quite frightened. "And then you can get on with your washing your own way. I might spoil your things or not do 'em as you like. I'm more used to gentlemen's things myself."

"Let you steer?" replied the barge woman, laughing. "It takes some practice to steer a barge properly. No, you shall do the washing you love to do. I'll stick to the steering that I understand."

Toad fetched tub, soap, and some brushes from the cabin. He picked up a few grimy garments. He tried to remember how other people washed clothes. And then he plunged in…

A long half-hour passed, and a burst of laughter made him look round. The barge woman was laughing wildly.

"I thought you must be a humbug from the conceited way you talked," she gasped. "I bet you've never washed a dishrag!"

"You common barge woman!" Toad shouted. "I would have you to know that I am a *Toad* and I will *not* be laughed at by a barge woman!"

"A horrid, nasty, crawly Toad!" she cried. "Now that is a thing that I will *not* have."

She grabbed Toad and threw him through the air. He landed in the water with a plop! Toad rose to the surface spluttering and saw the barge woman still laughing. He vowed, as he coughed and choked, to be even with her.

He struck out for the shore, gathering his wet skirts over his arms. He ran after the barge as fast as his legs would carry him, thirsting for revenge.

The barge woman was still laughing.

Toad reached the horse, untied him, jumped on his back, and galloped away, leaving the barge to drift to the other side. The Toad laughed a victor's laugh. He was a clever Toad!

Toad rode on, trying to forget how very long it was since he had eaten. Soon the canal was left far behind him.

He had traveled some miles, his horse and he, when he came upon a gypsy wagon. Beside the wagon was a man sitting on a bucket. Over a fire hung an iron pot. Out of that pot came smells—warm and rich. And he was *such* a hungry Toad.

The gypsy eyed him. "Want to sell that horse of yours?"

Toad was not expecting this. He could turn the horse into cash!

"What?" Toad said. "Me sell this beautiful young horse of mine? All the same, how much are you prepared to offer me for this horse?"

"Shillin' a leg," the man said briefly.

"A shilling a leg?" cried Toad. "Why, that comes to only four shillings for four legs. Oh, no, I could not think of taking only four shillings."

"Well," said the gypsy, "I'll make it five."

Then Toad sat and pondered deeply. For he was hungry and quite penniless. And he was still far away—how far he did not know—from home. And enemies might still be looking for him.

"Look here, gypsy! You hand me over six shillings and sixpence. And, you shall give me as much breakfast as I can possibly eat out of that iron pot of yours. In return, I will sell to you my spirited young horse."

The gypsy grumbled. But he counted out six shillings and sixpence and gave Toad as much stew as he could possibly eat.

With his pockets full of money and his tummy full of food, Toad tramped along merrily and thought about his wonderful luck. His pride and conceit began to swell within him. He got so puffed up with conceit that he made up a song in praise of himself and sang it at the top of his voice.

The world has held great Heroes,
    As history books have showed.
But never a name to go down to fame
    Compared with that of Toad!

The clever men at Oxford
    Know all that there is to be knowed.
But they none of them know one-half as much
    As intelligent Mr. Toad!

The animals sat in the Ark and cried,
    Their tears in torrents flowed.
Who was it said, "There's land ahead!"
    Encouraging Mr. Toad!

The army all saluted
    As they marched along the road.
Was it the King? Or a Kitchener?
    No. It was Mr. Toad.

The Queen and her Ladies-in-waiting
    Sat at the window and sewed.
She cried, "Look! Who's that handsome *man?"*
    They answered, "Mr. Toad."

After walking miles of country lanes, he saw something coming down the road. Then he heard something that made his heart stop. Toot-toot!

He stepped confidently into the road to stop the motorcar—when suddenly he realized it was the very same car that he had stolen! And the people in it were the very same people he had stolen it from! In fear, Toad sank down in a shabby, miserable heap in the road.

The motorcar stopped just short of him. Two gentlemen got out. One of them said, "Here is a poor old washerwoman! Perhaps she is overcome by the heat. Let's take her into the next town."

They tenderly lifted Toad into the motorcar and propped him up with soft cushions, and went on their way.

When Toad realized he had not been recognized, he slowly opened his eyes.

"Now, keep quite still," said one of the gentlemen, "and don't try to talk."

"I won't," said Toad. "I was only thinking that if I could sit in the front seat—by the driver—I might feel better with the wind in my face."

"Of course!" they said. So they helped Toad into the front seat and on they went again.

"I've been watching you carefully," Toad said to the driver. "I wish you would kindly let me drive the car for a little."

The driver laughed at this, but one of the gentlemen in the back said, "Let her have a try. She won't do any harm."

Toad scrambled into the driver's seat and set the car in motion. Slowly and carefully at first.

"How well she drives!" said the gentlemen.

Toad went a little faster. Then faster, FASTER!

"Be careful, washerwoman!"

"Washerwoman, indeed!" Toad shouted. "Ho! Ho! I am the Toad, the motorcar snatcher, Toad who always escapes! You are in the hands of the famous, the skillful, the fearless Toad!"

The men tried to grab the Toad. With a half-turn of the wheel the Toad sent the car crashing through a hedge and into a horse pond.

Toad flew through the air and landed with a thump in the soft rich grass of a meadow. He could just see the motorcar sitting in the pond.

He picked himself up and set off running across country as hard as he could. He giggled, and laughed, and sat down under a hedge. "Toad again! Clever Toad! How clever I am!" Then he sang out:

"The motorcar went Toot-toot-toot,
As it raced along the road.
Who was it steered it into a pond?
Ingenious Mr. Toad!"

A slight noise behind him made him turn his head and look. About two fields off, two large country policemen were running toward him!

Toad sprang to his feet and hurried away again. He glanced back and saw to his dismay that they were gaining on him. He could hear them close behind him now. He struggled on wildly, not watching where he was going. Suddenly the earth gave way under his feet, and *Splash!* he found himself in fast-moving water that carried him along with a force he could not fight. He knew that in his blind panic he had run straight into the river!

He rose to the surface and tried to grasp the reeds that grew along the water's edge. But the stream was so strong that it tore them out of his hands. Then down he went, and came up breathless and spluttering. Presently he saw a big dark hole in the bank, and as the stream carried him past he caught hold of the edge.

He sighed, blew his nose, and stared before him into the dark hole. Some bright small thing shone and twinkled deep within the hole—and it was moving toward him. Slowly, a face grew around it. A familiar face!

A brown face, with whiskers.

A round face with a twinkle in its eye.

With small neat ears and thick silky hair.

It was the Water Rat!

CHAPTER ELEVEN

The Fall of Toad Hall

The Rat put out a paw, gripped Toad firmly by the scruff of the neck, and gave a great pull.

"Oh, Ratty!" Toad cried, when safe inside the Rat's home. "I've been through such times since I saw you last! I tell you—"

"Toad," said the Water Rat, "you go upstairs at once, take off that dress, clean yourself up, put on some of my clothes, and try and come down looking like a gentleman!"

Toad was about to be huffy with the Rat. However, he caught sight of himself in the mirror over the hat stand. Seeing how badly he looked, he changed his mind and went quickly upstairs.

By the time he came down, lunch was on the table. While they ate, Toad told Rat all his adventures. But the more Toad talked, the more grave and silent the Rat became.

When at last Toad had talked himself to a standstill, there was silence for a while. Then the Rat said, "Now, Toady, don't you see what a fool you've been? Motorcars are just trouble for you."

"But I've had such fun! Awful fun! But I'm going to be a good Toad now. I've had enough of adventures, so I'll be off now for Toad Hall."

"Do you mean to say you haven't *heard*?"

"Heard what?" said Toad, turning rather pale.

"About the Stoats and Weasels? How they've taken Toad Hall?" cried the Rat. From the look on his face, Rat could tell that Toad had *not* heard.

"After you went to prison," Rat went on, "Mole and Badger told everyone you'd be back— somehow, someway. They stuck it out for you. They moved their things into Toad Hall, and slept there, and watched over the place—to have it all ready for you when you turned up. Well, one dark night Mole and Badger were sitting by the fire when a band of weasels, ferrets, and stoats— armed to the teeth—rushed in upon them from every side. Those evil beasts bruised Badger and Mole with sticks and turned them out into the cold and wet! And the Wild Wooders, who've been living in Toad Hall ever since, are telling everybody that they've come to stay for good."

"Oh, have they!" said Toad, seizing a stick.

"You'll only get into trouble!" warned the Rat.

But the Toad was off and there was no holding him. When he got near his front gate, a long yellow ferret holding a gun popped up from behind the fence. Toad dropped flat in the road and *Bang!* a bullet whistled over Toad's head.

The startled Toad scrambled to his feet and scampered off down the road as hard as he could.

Still, Toad would not give in. He got out Ratty's boat and set off rowing up the river toward Toad Hall. All seemed very peaceful, deserted, and quiet. He was just passing under the bridge when… *Crash!* a great stone, dropped from above by two stoats, smashed through the bottom of the boat.

"*What* did I tell you?" said the Rat when the Toad returned. "And now you've lost my boat and ruined that nice suit of clothes I lent you! Really, Toad, I wonder how you manage to keep any friends at all!"

The Toad saw at once how foolishly he had acted, and gave a full apology.

"Then my advice to you is this," said the good-natured Rat. "Mole and Badger—"

"Ah, of course, Mole and Badger," said Toad lightly. "What's become of them? I had forgotten all about them."

"While you were living so recklessly," answered the Rat, "those devoted animals have been camping out in the open in every sort of weather, watching over your house. They've been planning how to get your property back for you. You don't deserve to have such true and loyal friends, Toad, really!"

"It's true," sobbed Toad, shedding bitter tears. "Let me go out and find them, out into the cold dark night, and try—Hold on! Is supper ready? Come, Ratty, let's eat before it gets cold!"

They had just finished their meal, and Toad had fallen asleep and was snoring by the fire, when in walked Mr. Badger. "Welcome home, Toad!" he said. "This is a poor homecoming."

Almost immediately, in walked Mole. "Here's old Toad!" cried Mole. "Why, you must have managed to escape, you clever, intelligent Toad!"

The Rat pulled Mole by the elbow, but it was too late.

"Clever? Oh, no!" Toad said. "I'm a stupid mug, I am! I'll tell you a few of my little adventures, Mole, and you shall judge for yourself!"

"Toad, do be quiet!" said the Rat. "And don't you egg him on, Mole, when you know what he is. But please tell us what's best to be done now that Toad is back."

"Things aren't good," replied the Mole. "Guards posted everywhere, guns poked out at us, stones thrown at us, always an animal on the lookout. And when they see us, my! how they do laugh!"

"Toad!" Badger finally said. "You bad, troublesome little animal! I would expect to see you more ashamed of yourself. What do you think your father, my old friend, would have said if he had been here these last months and had known of all your goings on?"

Toad, who was on the sofa by this time, with his legs up, rolled over on his face, shaken by sobs of shame.

"Stop crying," went on the Badger more kindly. "What the Mole says about Toad Hall is quite true. It's useless to think of attacking the place."

"Then it's all over," sobbed the Toad. "I shall enlist in the Army, and never see my home again!"

"I haven't offered my last word yet," said the Badger. "I'll tell you a great secret."

Toad sat up slowly and dried his eyes.

"There—is—an—underground—passage," said the Badger, "that leads from the River Bank, quite near here, right up into the middle of Toad Hall."

"Oh, nonsense!" said Toad. "I know every inch of Toad Hall, inside and out, I do assure you!"

"Your father was a particular friend of mine," said the Badger sternly. "He told me a great deal he wouldn't have dreamed of telling you. He showed it to me. He said it was already there when he purchased the house."

"Then if it's there," Toad said, "a passage I've never seen, how's this passage of yours going to help us?"

"There's going to be a big banquet tomorrow night for the Chief Weasel's birthday," continued the Badger. "All the weasels will be gathered together in the dining hall, eating and drinking and laughing, suspecting nothing. No guns, no swords, no sticks, no weapons of any sort whatsoever!"

"But the lookouts will be posted as usual," remarked the Rat.

"Exactly," said the Badger. "That is my point. The weasels will completely trust their lookouts, the stoats. And that is where the passage comes in.

That very useful tunnel leads right up under the pantry next to the dining hall!"

"We shall creep out quietly into the pantry—" cried Mole.

"—with pistols and swords and sticks—" shouted the Rat.

"—and rush in upon them," said the Badger.

"—and whack 'em, and whack 'em!" cried the Toad, joyfully running round the room.

"Very well, then," said the Badger, "our plan is settled. It's getting late. Off to bed, now. We'll discuss matters in the morning."

When Toad came down for breakfast the next morning he found that Mole had already slipped off. Badger sat in the armchair reading the paper. Rat was running round, busily sorting out weapons in four little heaps on the floor.

The door opened and the Mole came tumbling into the room. "I've been having such fun!" he said with glee. "I've been messing with the stoats!"

"I hope you've been very careful, Mole," said the Rat anxiously.

"I should hope so, too," said the Mole confidently. "I got the idea when I went into the kitchen to make sure Toad's breakfast was being kept hot for him. I found that old washerwoman outfit—the dress, the bonnet, the shawl—that he came home in yesterday. So I put them on and off I went to Toad Hall. The stoats were on the lookout. 'Good morning, gentlemen!' says I, very respectful. 'Want any washing done today?' They looked at me very proud and stiff and haughty. The Sergeant in charge, he said to me, 'Now run away, my good woman!' 'Run away?' says I, 'It won't be *me* that'll be running away!' "

"Oh, *Moly*, how could you?" moaned the Rat.

The Badger laid down his paper.

The Mole went on. "The Sergeant said to them, 'Never mind *her*. She doesn't know what she's talking about.' 'Oh! Don't I?' said I. 'My daughter washes for Mr. Badger, and I know for a fact that a hundred bloodthirsty Badgers, armed with rifles, are going to attack Toad Hall this very night. Six boatloads of Rats, with pistols and swords, will come up the river and land in the garden. Meanwhile a select group of Toads, known as the Death-or-Glory Toads, will storm the orchard and carry everything before them. Were I you, I'd leave now.' They were all as nervous and flustered as could be."

"You've spoiled everything!" cried Toad.

"Mole," said the Badger quietly, "you did very *well*. Good Mole! Clever Mole!"

The Toad was simply wild with jealousy, more so because he had no idea what the Mole had done that was particularly clever.

After lunch, Badger took a nap.

Rat continued gathering weapons.

And Mole put his arm through Toad's, led him out into the open air, shoved him into a wicker chair, and made him tell him all his adventures from beginning to end, which Toad was only too willing to do.

CHAPTER TWELVE

The Return of Toad

When it began to grow dark, the Rat called them all back into the parlor. He stood each of them beside one of the little heaps of weapons. Then he dressed them for the coming battle.

When all was ready, the Badger took a lantern in one paw, grasped his great stick with the other and said, "Now then, follow me! Mole first, Rat next, Toad last. Toady! Don't chatter!"

The Badger led them along the river, and then suddenly swung himself over the edge into a hole, a little above the water. The Mole and the Rat followed. Toad, of course, managed to slip and fall into the water with a loud splash.

The tunnel was cold, dark, damp, and low. Poor Toad began to shiver. The lantern was far ahead and he could not help lagging behind in the darkness. The terror of being left behind seized him and he ran forward with such a rush that he upset the Rat into the Mole and the Mole into the Badger. The Badger thought they were being attacked. He drew a pistol and almost shot Toad.

Then, suddenly, they heard, sounding far up over their heads, a confused murmur of sound.

The passage now began to slope upward. The sound of laughter and applause broke out, this time very close above them. "*What* a time those weasels are having!" said the Badger. They hurried along till they found themselves under the trapdoor that led up into the pantry.

The Badger said, "Now, all together!" Hoisting each other up, they found themselves standing in the pantry with only a door between them and their unsuspecting enemies.

"Our thanks to *clever* Toad!" a weasel laughed.

"Just let me at him," muttered Toad.

The Badger drew himself up, and shouted—

"The hour is come!"

—and flung the door open wide.

What a squealing, a squeaking, and a screeching filled the air!

Weasels dived under tables and sprang for the windows! Ferrets ran for the fireplace and jammed the chimney! Tables and chairs were upset! And glass and china crashed to the floor as the Heroes strode into the room! They were only four in all, but to the panic-stricken weasels the hall seemed full of monstrous animals, whooping and waving enormous weapons.

The battle was soon over as terrified weasels shrieked across the lawn. On the floor lay a dozen or so of the enemy who did not escape. The Mole was busily fitting handcuffs on them.

"Mole," Badger said, "you're the best of fellows! Slip outside and check on the stoat lookouts. I've an idea that, thanks to you, we won't have much trouble from *them* tonight!"

Toad felt rather hurt that the Badger didn't say pleasant things to him as he had to the Mole, and tell him what a fine fellow he was, and how splendidly he had fought. For Toad was quite pleased with the way he himself had gone after the Chief Weasel and sent him flying across the table.

Mole returned through the window, chuckling.

"From what I can tell," he reported, "even the stoats threw down their rifles and fled. They've *all* disappeared by now!"

"Excellent animal!" said the Badger. "Now, there's just one more thing. I want you to take those fellows on the floor there upstairs with you and have some bedrooms cleaned out. See that they sweep *under* the beds and put clean sheets and pillowcases on. And then, put them out by the backdoor. I'm very pleased with you, Mole!"

The following morning, Toad had overslept as usual. He came down to breakfast and found nothing to eat. This did not improve his temper. After all, it was his *own* house. Through the windows of the breakfast room he could see the Mole and the Rat sitting out on the lawn. The Badger, who was in an armchair, remarked rather shortly, "I'm sorry, Toad, but I'm afraid there's a heavy morning's work in front of you. We really ought to have a Banquet at once to celebrate this affair. It's expected of you—in fact, it's the rule. If we have the Banquet tonight, the invitations will have to be written and sent at once. Now, sit down at that table and write to all our friends. *I'll* lend a hand, too. *I'll* order the Banquet."

"What?" cried Toad. "Me stay indoors and write a lot of rotten letters! I'll be—! Er—Why, of course, dear Badger! You wish it done, and it shall be done."

The Badger looked at him with suspicion, then left the room. As soon as the door had closed, Toad hurried to the writing table. A fine idea had occurred to him while he was talking. He would write the invitations. And he *would* take care to mention the leading part he had taken in the fight. And he would include a program of entertainment for the evening—something like this, as he sketched it out in his head:

SPEECH .... BY TOAD
(There will be other speeches by TOAD later.)

ADDRESS .... BY TOAD
Our Prison System—The Waterways of England
Horse-dealing—On Being an English Squire

SONG .... BY TOAD
(*Composed by himself*)

OTHER COMPOSITIONS .... BY TOAD
Sung in the evening by the ...... COMPOSER

Toad worked very hard on his letters. He got a weasel to help deliver them, and he had sent out all the invitations by noon.

When the other animals came back, Badger and Rat caught Toad by the arm.

"Now, look here, Toad," said the Rat. "It's about this Banquet. We know you too well. We want you to understand clearly, once and for all, that there are to be *no* speeches and *no* songs."

"Can't I sing them just one *little* song?" Toad pleaded with sorrow in his eyes.

"No, not *one* little song," replied the Rat. "You know well that your songs are all conceit and your speeches are all self-praise. It's for your own good, Toady."

Toad at last raised his head. "It was but a small thing—merely to hear the great applause that—brings out my best qualities!" And pressing his handkerchief to his face, he left the room.

"It's lucky we came upon that little weasel just as he was setting out with Toad's invitations," said the Rat. "They were simply disgraceful. Fortunately, Mole has agreed to write out new invitation cards."

"Good Mole," said Badger proudly.

At last the hour for the Banquet began to draw near. Toad had gone up to his bedroom to pout. After a while, however, he began giggling shyly to himself. He got up, locked the door and drew the curtains across the windows. Then he set up all the chairs in the room in front of him, like an audience, and began to sing, loudly and with great gusto:

TOAD'S LAST LITTLE SONG!

The Toad—came—home!
There was panic in the parlor
and howling in the hall,
There was crying in the cowshed
and shrieking in the stall,
When the Toad—came—home!

When the Toad—came—home!
There was smashing in of window
and crashing in of door,
There was pestering of weasels
that fainted on the floor,
When the Toad—came—home!

Bang! go the drums!
The trumpeters are tooting
  and the soldiers are saluting,
And the cannon they are shooting
  and the motorcars are tooting,
As the—Hero—comes!

Shout—Hoo-ray!
And let each one of the crowd try
  and shout it very loud,
In honor of an animal
  of whom you're justly proud,
For it's Toad's—great—day!

He sang it all over again. Then he heaved a deep sigh—a long, long, long sigh.

And then he parted his hair in the middle, slicked it down, unlocked the door, and went quietly down the stairs to greet his guests.

All the animals cheered when Toad entered. They crowded round to congratulate him and say nice things about his courage, his cleverness, and his fighting qualities. But Toad only smiled and murmured, "Oh, it was nothing. Oh, please, really. Not at all!"

Otter came forward with a shout and threw his arm round Toad's neck. Toad only remarked gently, "Badger was the mastermind. The Mole and Water Rat bore the brunt of the fighting. I merely served in the ranks and did little or nothing."

The animals were puzzled by this unexpected attitude of his. Toad rather liked this new kind of attention. He moved from one guest to the other, making his modest responses, and thus everyone now found him to be very interesting.

The Badger had ordered only the best, and the Banquet was a great success. There was much talking, laughter, and joking among the animals. But through it all, Toad only murmured polite comments to the animals on either side of him. He never once remarked on himself. Badger and Rat were in shock at Toad's mannerly behavior, and this gave Toad the greatest satisfaction of all. There were some knockings on the table and cries of "Toad! Speech! Speech from Toad! Song! Mr. Toad's song!" But Toad only shook his head gently, raised one paw, and smiled, asking his guests to eat and enjoy themselves. It was a Banquet for them, not him.

He was indeed an altered Toad!

After this, the four animals led their lives in great joy, respect, and contentment.

Toad selected a handsome gold chain and locket set with pearls that he mailed to the jailer's daughter with a letter of thanks. Even the Badger admitted that this was a kind, thoughtful thing for Toad to do. Toad also wrote to properly thank the engine driver. He sent him some money for all his pains and trouble.

Under severe pressure from Badger, Toad even found out where the barge woman was, and sent her money for the horse he had stolen from her.

A lawyer got all charges against Toad dropped, in exchange for time already served in prison—and because Toad had truly become a more mannerly Toad.

Everyone had now been rewarded for his or her part.

Sometimes, during long summer evenings, the friends would take a stroll together in the Wild Wood, now tamed. It was pleasing to see how nicely they were greeted by the animals who lived there. The mother weasels would bring their young ones to the doors of their dens and say, pointing, "Look, baby! There goes the great Mr. Toad! And that's the gallant Water Rat, a terrible fighter, walking alongside o' him! And yonder comes the famous Mr. Mole. You've often heard your father tell of him!"

But when their children were irritable and quite beyond control, they would quiet them by telling how, if they didn't hush, the terrible gray Badger would come and get them.

This was not true at all about the Badger. For, though he did not care much about Society, he *was* rather fond of children. But the mother weasels' words never failed to have their full effect.

The End

KENNETH GRAHAME

Kenneth Grahame was born in Edinburgh, Scotland, in 1859. His mother died when he was young, and his father left the children, who went to live with their grandmother. This sad beginning did have a happy result. Kenneth's grandmother lived in a lovely area near the Thames River and Windsor Forest. It was this beautiful, magical place that sparked the young boy's imagination and became a part of his future writings.

Grahame went into banking, but he loved writing. His first novels, *Dream Days* (1895) and *The Golden Age* (1898), spoke of the romance of childhood, and were very popular.

Grahame married and had one son, Alastair, who was partially blind. In 1908, Grahame wrote the spirited yet dream-like book *The Wind in the Willows*, in part as a present to his son. The book was a success, and continues to be loved by readers—young and old—to this day.

In his last years, Grahame lived in a quaint town by the side of the Thames River, much like the animal friends in his beloved novel. He died in 1932.